David Melling

DON'T WORRY, HUGLESS DOUGLAS

A division of Hachette Children's Books

Hodder Children's Books

Douglas and his dad were playing.
    'What's behind your back?' asked Douglas.
'Not that hand, the other one.'
Dad smiled,
'Something for you!'

It was a new woolly hat.

'Wow!' said Douglas.
'Thanks, Dad.'
Douglas had never
had a woolly
hat before.
He couldn't wait
to show his friends.

'Look after it,' said Dad.

But Douglas was already off!

'Look at me!' shouted Douglas.

'Snazzy hat, Douglas!'
baaed the sheep.

OOF!

'I can even do cartwheels in it!' he whooped.
And he did. Again. And again.

Until something didn't feel right.

Douglas gasped. His new woolly hat had turned into one long string of spaghetti!

'That's not supposed to happen,' he gulped.
'Don't worry, Douglas,' said the sheep.
'We'll fix it.'
They wound it into a ball and squished it
back into shape.

'Any good?' they asked.
'**NO!**' said Douglas.

'Cow is a good
thinker,' said
the sheep.
'She'll know
what to do.'

Cow thought she had a very good idea.
'Pretty!' she said.

'**NO**,' said Douglas.

'Don't worry, Douglas!' chirped a swoopy bird,
'I can use this for my nest.'

'NO, YOU CAN'T,'
yelped Douglas.
'That's my new woolly hat!'

'Doesn't look like a woolly hat,'
said the swoopy bird.
'Anyway,' he puffed,
'it doesn't fit.'
And he dropped it out of the tree.

Just then it began to rain.

Douglas was really
worried now.
    'What's my dad going
        to say?' he mumbled.

Rabbit popped up. 'Ooh, thanks Douglas.
Just what I need to plug the hole in my burrow.'
'**THAT'S MY NEW WOOLLY HAT!**'
cried Douglas.

'My dad gave it to me.'

'Sorry,' said Rabbit, 'I didn't know.
Come here,' she said and wiped his nose.

'What am I going to do?' sniffed Douglas.

Rabbit looked thoughtful.

'Why don't you just tell your dad what happened? He's nice, your dad, he'll understand.'

Maybe Rabbit was right. Douglas picked up his wet spaghetti hat and trudged back home.

'Oh, Douglas,' sighed his mum.
'Look at you!'

'Where's your new hat?' asked his dad.

Douglas told them everything.

'Don't worry, Douglas,' said Dad.
'I've got something for you.
Guess which hand?'
Douglas wasn't sure.
'Here's my hat,' laughed Dad.

'You'll soon grow into it!'

Banana Hat

Nappy Hat

I Don't Like Peas Hat

Follow-The-Leader Hat

Spot-The-Difference Hat

Best Friends Hat

Pants Hat

Peek-a-Boo Hat

Wig Hat

Weather Hat

Potty Hat

Love Hat

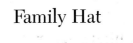

Family Hat

NEW!

A fun, interactive App.

DON'T WORRY, HUGLESS DOUGLAS
by David Melling

First published in 2011 by Hodder Children's Books

Text copyright © David Melling 2011
Illustration copyright © David Melling 2011

Hodder Children's Books
338 Euston Road
London NW1 3BH

Hodder Children's Books Australia
Level 17/207 Kent Street
Sydney NSW 2000

A catalogue record of this book is
available from the British Library.

ISBN: 978 0 340 99981 3
10 9 8 7 6

Printed in China

Hodder Children's Books
is a division of Hachette
Children's Books.
An Hachette UK Company.

www.hachette.co.uk